BABY BEAR'S

Book of Tiny Tales

DAVID McPHAIL

LITTLE, BROWN AND COMPANY

New York   Boston

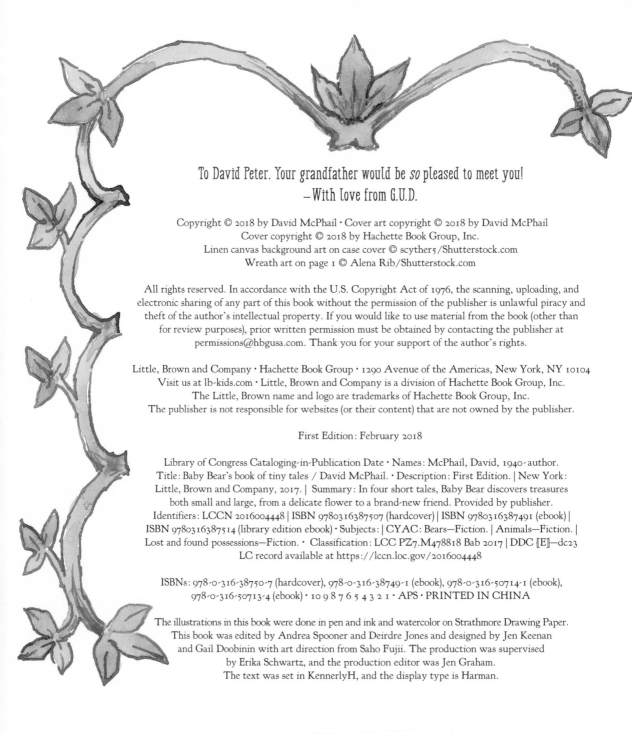

To David Peter. Your grandfather would be *so* pleased to meet you!
—With love from G.U.D.

Little, Brown and Company · Hachette Book Group · 1290 Avenue of the Americas, New York, NY 10104
Visit us at lb-kids.com · Little, Brown and Company is a division of Hachette Book Group, Inc.
The Little, Brown name and logo are trademarks of Hachette Book Group, Inc.
The publisher is not responsible for websites (or their content) that are not owned by the publisher.

First Edition: February 2018

Library of Congress Cataloging-in-Publication Date · Names: McPhail, David, 1940- author.
Title: Baby Bear's book of tiny tales / David McPhail. · Description: First Edition. | New York:
Little, Brown and Company, 2017. | Summary: In four short tales, Baby Bear discovers treasures
both small and large, from a delicate flower to a brand-new friend. Provided by publisher.
Identifiers: LCCN 2016004448 | ISBN 9780316387507 (hardcover) | ISBN 9780316387491 (ebook) |
ISBN 9780316387514 (library edition ebook) · Subjects: | CYAC: Bears—Fiction. | Animals—Fiction. |
Lost and found possessions—Fiction. · Classification: LCC PZ7.M478818 Bab 2017 | DDC [E]—dc23
LC record available at https://lccn.loc.gov/2016004448

ISBNs: 978-0-316-38750-7 (hardcover), 978-0-316-38749-1 (ebook), 978-0-316-50714-1 (ebook),
978-0-316-50713-4 (ebook) · 10 9 8 7 6 5 4 3 2 1 · APS · PRINTED IN CHINA

The illustrations in this book were done in pen and ink and watercolor on Strathmore Drawing Paper.
This book was edited by Andrea Spooner and Deirdre Jones and designed by Jen Keenan
and Gail Doobinin with art direction from Saho Fujii. The production was supervised
by Erika Schwartz, and the production editor was Jen Graham.
The text was set in KennerlyH, and the display type is Harman.

Baby Bear Finds a Boot

Baby Bear was fishing. He did not catch a fish.
Instead, he caught a boot.

"Someone has lost a boot," thought Baby Bear.
"I must give it back."

He walked along the riverbank carrying the boot until he
saw his friend Timmy Squirrel.

"I caught a boot," said Baby Bear. "Is it yours?"

"Not mine," said Timmy Squirrel. "It's the wrong color!"

Baby Bear kept walking. He saw his friend Bobby Raccoon.

"Hello, Bobby," said Baby Bear. "Is this your boot?"

Bobby Raccoon looked closely.

"No, it's not mine," he said. "It's too big."

Next, Baby Bear showed the boot to Daisy Skunk.
"Not mine," she told him. "I don't wear boots!"

Ollie Owl flew down and landed on a nearby branch.
"What are you doing with that boot, Baby Bear?" he asked.

"I'm trying to find out who lost it," answered Baby Bear.

"Hoo?" said Ollie.

"Yes, *who*!" said Baby Bear. "If you can think of *who*, please let me know."

"Hoo!" Ollie called, as he disappeared into the treetops.

"Hoo! Hoo! Hoo!"

Baby Bear was getting very tired. Would he ever find the owner of the boot?

Then he saw someone sitting at the edge of the river. It was Papa Bear, and he was fast asleep. Papa Bear's feet were dangling in the water, and he was wearing just *one* boot.

"Wake up, Papa!" said Baby Bear. "I found your boot!"

"So you did, Baby Bear," said Papa Bear. "It must have fallen off and floated away."

Papa Bear spread his arms for a hug. "Thank you for finding it."

"You're welcome, Papa," said Baby Bear.

Baby Bear Finds a Flower

Baby Bear was walking in the woods when he saw a beautiful flower.

"I will take this beautiful flower home to Mama Bear," he thought.

Baby Bear reached down to pick the flower.

"Stop!" someone cried.

It was his friend Daisy Skunk.

"Do not pick that flower," Daisy told him. "It is *rare*."

"What is *rare*?" asked Baby Bear.

"It means that this flower could be the only one left in the whole world," said Daisy.

"Oh dear," said Baby Bear. "But I wanted to take it home to Mama Bear."

Baby Bear and Daisy Skunk sat down beside the flower. They were quiet for a long time.

Then Daisy jumped up.

"I have the answer!" she cried. "You can't take the flower
to Mama Bear, so bring Mama Bear to the flower."

"What a good idea, Daisy," Baby Bear called over his shoulder, as he ran to find Mama Bear.

Mama Bear was painting a picture outside their den.

"Come quick, Mama!" said Baby Bear. "I have something
to show you."

"What is it, Baby Bear?" she asked.

"It is a surprise!" said Baby Bear.

"Here we are, Mama," said Baby Bear, when they reached the flower.

Mama Bear looked around, but all she saw was Daisy Skunk.

"Hello, Daisy. It is nice to see you," said Mama Bear.

"But it is not a surprise."

"I am not the surprise," said Daisy. "*This* is!"

Daisy stepped aside to reveal the beautiful flower.
"Oh, what a wonderful surprise!" said Mama Bear.
She hugged them both and leaned down to smell
the flower.

"I am so glad that you didn't pick this flower," said
Mama Bear. "It is very rare."

Baby Bear and Daisy Skunk smiled at each other.

"We know," they said.

Baby Bear Finds a Baby Bird

Baby Bear was sitting under a tree when he heard a "cheep!"
A baby bird was sitting on the ground next to him.

"What are you doing out of your nest?" asked Baby Bear.

"I leaned too far over the edge," said the baby bird.
"I fell out!"

"Oh dear," said Baby Bear. "What will you do now?"

"My mother will be home soon," answered the
baby bird. "She will come and get me."

Suddenly, a dark shadow passed over them.
It was a hawk!

Baby Bear knew that hawks were no friends of
baby birds. He stood up and waved his arms and
growled as loudly as he could. The hawk looked
at Baby Bear and then flew away.

"I think I should wait here with you until your mother comes," said Baby Bear.

They waited and waited.

Finally the baby bird's mother arrived.

"Oh, my baby!" she cried. "Climb on my back,
and I will fly you up to the nest."

The baby bird did as she was told. But when her mother tried to fly, she couldn't! As small as she was, the baby bird was just too heavy.

The mother was upset. "What will we do now?"
she wondered. "You can't stay here."

"I have an idea!" said Baby Bear.

Baby Bear gently placed the baby bird on his head
and started to climb the tree.

Up he went . . . slowly, carefully, steadily . . . and soon
he reached the nest.

Baby Bear tipped his head down, and the baby bird
slid right in with a *plop*.

"Thank you so much!" said the baby bird's mother.

"That was fun!" said the baby bird. "Can we do
it again?"

"No, we cannot," said Baby Bear. "But when you learn to fly, maybe you could come visit me."

"I would like that," said the baby bird, as Baby Bear climbed down the tree and headed home . . . but not before he waved to the baby bird one more time.

Baby Bear Finds a Friend

Baby Bear wanted someone to play with him. He went looking for his friend Timmy Squirrel, but Timmy was not at home.

"He is out collecting acorns with his father," said Timmy's mother.

Next, Baby Bear went to find his friend Bobby Raccoon,
but Bobby was sleeping. Being a raccoon, Bobby did most
of his playing at night.

Then Baby Bear went to Daisy Skunk's house.

"Daisy is having her drum lesson now," said Daisy's
mother. "Perhaps she will play with you later."

Baby Bear was sad. He had no one to play with him. Even Ollie Owl was not at home.

Then he heard someone talking. No, it was *two* people talking!

Wait! Maybe it was *three* . . . or even *four*!

Baby Bear stepped into a small clearing and was surprised
to see just one little girl having a picnic with her toys.

"Hello," the little girl said to Baby Bear. "Are you looking for someone?"

"Yes," said Baby Bear. "I am looking for a friend to play with me."

"These are my friends," said the little girl, introducing her toys to Baby Bear. "And my name is Julia."

"I am pleased to meet you all," said Baby Bear. "I am Baby Bear."

Julia looked at Baby Bear. "Maybe we can be your new friends. Would you like to help us eat our sandwiches?"

"Yes, I would like that very much!" said Baby Bear.

So the new friends ate the sandwiches and drank tea together.

"I hope you are not too full," said Julia.

"Why?" Baby Bear asked.

"Because now that we are friends, I can tell you a secret," she whispered.

"We are having cake for dessert!"
"Can we have some cake, too?" a voice called.

It was Timmy Squirrel with Bobby Raccoon,
Daisy Skunk, and Ollie Owl!

"These are my friends," said Baby Bear, introducing them to Julia. "May they join us?"

"Of course," said Julia. "Let's all be friends!"

THE END